THE TRIP OF A LIFETIME

JUSTIN JOHNSON

CCS
Publishing

"You're going where?!"

My mother stood in the kitchen, exasperated by what I'd just told her. Her hand moved from the spoon she'd been stirring the tomato sauce with to her hip.

My father walked up behind her and put his hand on her shoulder. "Not a chance," he said. "Evan, it's the week before Christmas."

"I know, but I really want to," I argued. "I mean, I've been to eight of the nine planets so far and going to the ninth just before Christmas would be the best present I could get."

"No," my mother fired back. "Not a chance. It's too dangerous."

"And besides," my father added, "didn't you say that

the last time you took your ship out that you almost didn't make it home?"

"Sure," I said. "I had a few issues the last time, but I've fixed everything. I swear. Everything'll be fine. I'll be home before Christmas, I promise."

My mother pursed her lips and shook her head no, and my father followed suit.

I walked over to the dinner table and started to do my homework while I waited for dinner. I was so mad that I broke three pencil leads on the same problem. Not that I could really focus on what I was doing anyway. Thankfully, I was using a mechanical pencil so my parents couldn't tell that I had broken anything.

They just didn't understand.

If I could make it to my ninth planet before I even turned nine, that would be some kind of a record. And I know that some people don't even call Pluto a planet anymore, but that doesn't matter to me. It was a planet when I was born, it'll be a planet when I get to it.

As my mother returned to stirring her sauce and my father went back to the living room to sit in his recliner, I began plotting my journey.

hat night, after my parents had tucked me in and I was sure they were in bed, I cracked my window open slowly.

The frosty air of December nipped my nose a little and gave me a start. I jumped back, the breath from my lungs taken from me for a moment.

As I looked out over the window, a sense of dread filled me. I'd never actually attempted an escape before and the thought of jumping down two stories to the snow covered ground below had my stomach in knots.

I took a deep breath and reached for the side of my window, putting my foot on the base and pulling myself out into the cold. If I had thought the air was cold from inside my room, it was as if I'd been catapulted into a freezer once I was outside. I could feel my nose hairs sticking together, and ripping apart with every breath I took. At first, it hurt a tad. But after a while I got used to it, and actually felt myself enjoying it in some weird way.

It was mid-December and it had been a 'wicked' winter so far. That's what my dad had said, anyway. To be fair, he had done more than his fair share of snow blowing and shoveling since Thanksgiving.

And the way my room was positioned in the house, the area just below my window had some massive banks built up.

The way I looked at it, if I didn't go straight through the snow and get buried below it, I'd be able to roll right off onto the driveway, giving me a clear run to the garage.

Without much thought I went for it — Just jumped right off my windowsill. You should know that I'm a pretty small kid. I'm in the fourth grade, but I'd be considered small for a second grader. Normally, this was something the other kids picked on me about. But in moments like this it worked to my advantage.

I was able to land with a small thud, which hurt a little, but not too much, and then nimbly roll off the snow bank and onto the driveway.

When I'd gotten to my feet, two things hit me. One was how quiet it was out here. It was as if the very sound of my feet crunching in the newly fallen snow on the driveway might wake my parents out of a sound sleep. The other was the wind, which was whistling softly. It was just like I'd imagine one of those pictures from a kid's story book to be — the ones that have the man in the cloud blowing the wind over the new fallen snow.

And upon feeling the wind, I remembered that I had left my jacket up in my room. And there was no way I was going to be able to get it back now. Not if I wanted to give Pluto a run and get back before Christmas.

So, without further ado, I jogged to the garage and threw open the door and started to drag my spaceship from its stall.

3

$\mathcal{M}$y father had been right about one thing. The last time I took my ship out, I almost hadn't made it home. It malfunctioned somewhere around Neptune and gave me trouble almost the whole way back.

I'd told my parents about it, and regretted that decision instantly. They hemmed and hawed and were emphatically trying to talk me out of going anywhere else until I could get a new ship.

"Where am I supposed to get one? I don't have any money!" I'd asked argumentatively.

This was back in October and my parents had so flippantly suggested that I write it on my Christmas list and ask Santa for one.

Upon hearing this, I ended the conversation as I

thought that a new spaceship might be too tall an order for Santa. After all, I'd gotten mine from a Child Behavioral Specialist named Zebo from a planet called Threa in another galaxy. He'd left his with me when he found out how interested in space exploration I was.

When I asked him how he was going to get back to his family, he just winked and smiled and said, "Evan, don't you worry about a thing. I'll just catch a ride home with Xanther in a few months."

Ever since then, I've had my own rocket ship. It was a little small, but as I've already mentioned, so am I. So it worked out pretty perfectly.

Except now, it was a tad bit broken. Don't get me wrong, it wasn't broken enough to keep me home. But I'm a kid and my decision making is suspect at best. I realize that now. But I didn't realize it then.

I threw back the door and hopped in. I pressed the igniter switch and watched as a blue flame came out the back.

I then closed the door and rubbed my hands together in front of my mouth while I tried to warm them with my breath. A few more minutes and the heat would kick on, but I still had to steer this puppy out of the driveway and up into the atmosphere.

As I was leaving the garage, I caught a glimpse of my parents.

They were standing on the back porch. They hadn't

even had time to put on their robes. And for the first time on this journey, I felt a sadness. It was deep and strong. I knew I was letting them down and I knew they wouldn't see me for at least a week. And worst of all, I knew they'd be worried sick about me.

But I had to go. I just had to.

Pluto was calling my name and if I didn't get there before Christmas, it would be a strong possibility that I'd never make it there at all.

I saw my mother cover her mouth and press her face against my father's chest. And I saw my father hold her tight, no doubt telling her I'd be alright, hoping that it wasn't just some empty promise.

And then I was off, my ship warmed up and shooting into the sky like the rocket that it was. And I saw the shape of my mother and father become as tiny as a pin, and my home was as small as a dime.

I wiped the tears from my eyes and got ready for the trip of a lifetime.

4

*I*t wasn't long and I was way up into the atmosphere, chomping at the bit to get up into space and heading toward Pluto. I just knew this was going to be amazing.

And then something happened. It started with the gauges. They started going all wonky and I couldn't figure out what was going on. They were spinning uncontrollably and a red light had started flashing inside the cabin.

I did what any untrained space traveler would do: I hit the dash uncontrollably and started blurting out random incoherent curses.

A few seconds after this started, I felt my stomach suddenly come up and move toward my throat. I hadn't felt this sick since I was on that roller coaster last summer with my dad and we'd gone up the big hill and then we started on the way — DOWN!!!!

That's right! I was heading down toward the ground. And at this point all of the controls of my ship were unresponsive and useless.

My parents were right. That's what I found myself thinking as I plummeted toward the ground.

My odds of surviving this were low, that I knew. But I continued to look for anything that might give me an idea of where I was.

And then I saw them — the Northern Lights!

They were beautiful throughout the sky, streaks of greens and purples and reds and golds. The Aurora Borealis. There were worse sights to see as you were falling to your death.

With that, I sat back and tried my best to enjoy the last few moments of my life.

And then the ground was getting closer.

Panic set in.

And then the front of my ship made contact with the snow.

Glass surrounding me shattered.

And then I felt the cold.

Then things went black and I felt nothing at all.

5

I could hear them.

Not see them.

A few of them. Maybe four or five. Whispering.

"Do you think he's ever going to wake up?"

"What's the hurry? His vital signs are good."

"The boss said he wanted to see him when things were good."

"But he's not awake yet, you nincompoop."

I could feel my eyes start to peel themselves apart. My head was pounding and I was quite groggy.

Once my eye lids had finally separated, I was shocked at what I saw. And if I hadn't met Zebo a few years back, I would have never guessed that such things could ever exist.

There were four men, both young and old standing

around my bed. They were small. In fact, they were so small that if I would have been able to stand up, not a one of them would have been as tall as me.

All of them were wearing green felt jackets and pants, with peppermint candy cane striped stockings that led down into black boots with big gold buckles that curled up at the toes and had a bell on the end. They had thick black belts around their sizable bellies. And on top of their heads, they wore little red hats.

The two older ones had long white beards and wisps of white hair rolling out around the brim of their hats. The two younger ones were clean shaven with short hair, that appeared to be perfectly combed beneath their caps. One had jet black hair and the other a yellow that was so yellow there was no way I could call it blond.

"Well, there he is," said one of the older ones, holding out his hand as if showing me off to a crowded theater. "The boss will want to see him now."

"Calm down a little, Duffy," said the other old one. "The boy needs a meal and some time to get acquainted with his new surroundings. This is obviously quite a shock for him."

I felt myself nodding agreement. He was absolutely right. I was hungry and I was confused.

He turned to me and said, "My boy, please allow me to introduce myself." He extended his hand and I shook it. "My name is Benny. I'm the second in command around here. And this," he motioned to the other one with white hair, "this is Duffy." And then he put his hand up to his mouth and spoke to me from behind it, as if telling a secret, "He wishes he was second in command."

He said this a little louder than perhaps he had meant to.

Duffy became visibly upset and said, "Fine, Benny. If this is the impression of the North Pole that you wish to give the boy, than so be it. But I will not sit here and be the butt of your jokes." And then Duffy turned on his heel and stormed out of the room with his nose in the air.

"Ah, don't worry about him," Benny said. "He's always been a little too sensitive so long as I've known him. He'll get over it in a day or two."

As interested as I was in Benny and Duffy and the other two individuals standing at my bedside, I couldn't quite get past something that Duffy had said on the way out. Had I heard him correctly when he'd said, "North Pole?" Could I really be on the North Pole?

And if I was on the North Pole, then these people standing around me were...

"We're the elves," Benny said. "Look...Evan, is it?"

I nodded.

"I can see the shock on your face. It's okay, we're just like anybody else, except that our day job is making toys for the big man."

"Yeah," chimed in the elf with the yellow hair. Extending his hand, he said, "I'm Herbie, by the way. You're going to love it here."

"But you're going to be busy as soon as we get some food into you and send you off to see the boss," said the elf with the black hair.

"Now, now Bart, let Evan adjust to things before we start throwing him into everything," Benny stepped in.

I was thankful that Benny was there with the others. It was easy to see why he was second in command. And then it occurred to me that if I was on the North Pole, surrounded by elves, all talking about the 'big man' or the 'boss,' then the first in command must be...

6

"Santa will be very pleased to meet you Evan. He's heard all about your exploits in space, and though he flies around the world in one night on a sleigh pulled by magical reindeer, he's always secretly wanted to go to space."

Benny was walking me through a corridor that was decorated with colorful lights, and tinsel interweaved with pine twigs. The smell of cinnamon and nutmeg were strong in the air, making me think of my mother's home made apple and pumpkin pies...and egg nog.

When we arrived at the end of the corridor there was a small door that was large enough for an elf to get through, but not much more.

"So, where are we going?" I mustered up the courage to ask.

"To the boss man's house."

I stopped dead in my tracks. How could this be happening? I'd made easily the biggest mistake in my life and somehow I was being rewarded with a trip to Santa Claus's house.

I gave my arm a little pinch.

Benny raised and eyebrow and said, "What are you doing?"

"I just can't believe this is all real. I was pinching myself to make sure I wasn't dreaming."

"Oh, trust me," Benny said, "This is all real. And when Santa's done speaking with you, I'm sure you'll understand just how real this is."

And for the first time, things started to feel a little less than whimsical.

"What do you mean?" I asked.

"Well, that's not really for me to say," answered Benny. "Just that it's not going to be all goody goody gum drops for you this week. You're here under some naughty pretenses. And Santa don't put up with naughty all that well."

"But I —"

"Save it Evan," Benny interrupted. "You picked a real doozy of a week to pull what you did. This is the week that Santa checks his list twice, making last minute adjustments to who's naughty and who's nice. And based on the last twenty four hours, I'd say that your name is in danger of sliding its way onto the naughty list, if it's not there already."

I didn't have time to argue, or even really comprehend what he was saying to me before he reached for the handle of the door and pulled it open and said, "Save it for Santa, sonny. We're here."

7

The door opened and the smell of pine and Christmas cookies wafted up my nose.

Benny stood outside the door and said, "After you."

I stepped inside the room and the first thing I noticed was that everything resembled crushed red velvet. The walls were a dark crimson color, and the carpet matched.

It was soft beneath my feet as I moved toward the massive mahogany desk on the opposite wall. As I approached, I was staring at the back of a chair. It too was red and looked like the softest chair I'd ever seen.

Benny stepped past me and walked around the desk. He leaned into the chair and whispered something to the person sitting in it.

A deep, booming voice spoke up and said, "Very well. Thank you, Benny."

Benny nodded and walked back around the desk. Before he left the room, he stopped in front of me for a moment and heaved a sigh and sent an eyebrow raise in my direction. I'd known I was in trouble before this look, but upon seeing Benny's face, the feeling of dread grew stronger within me.

"Good luck, kid," Benny said. And then he moved past me and closed the door after he left.

I brought my attention to the chair behind the desk and waited for my punishment. Slowly, the chair began to swivel and turn.

I could see a red shirt and green tie, and black suspenders. There was a white beard resting on the top of the tie and the mouth the beard was attached to was chewing on something. The man gave a throat clearing cough and then picked up a paper on his desk and held it in front of his bespectacled eyes.

He cleared his throat again as he examined the page.

"Not good," he said in a soft voice. "Most definitely not good."

He looked past the paper, directly at me.

I felt myself shrink.

The white bearded man motioned toward the chair I was standing next to and invited me to sit down. "We're going to be here a while," he said.

Slowly, I sat down and tried to find a comfortable position. But this chair was a little harder than I thought it would be. Or maybe, I was just in an uncomfortable situation. Whatever it was, I found myself squirming, hoping he wouldn't notice.

But of course, he knows everything. And so he noticed my squirming.

"Would it be possible for you to sit still?" he asked. "Or would you be more comfortable standing?"

I nodded.

"Well, which one, sonny boy?"

"St-st-standing," I stammered. And then, realizing I was in danger of sounding impolite, I stuttered, "p-p-plea-please."

"Of course," the man said, and moved his hand upward, indicating to me that it would be just fine if I got out of the chair and stood before him.

"This is very serious what you've done," he said. And then he looked over the golden rims of his glasses and called me by name. "Evan."

I swallowed hard and rubbed my sweaty hands on my pants before putting them back together again in front of my waist.

"What do you have to say for yourself?"

I shrugged my shoulders, not wanting to speak again. My tongue felt like it was triple its normal size and the idea of having to stammer and sputter through everything I wanted to say was mortifying.

"A shrug?" the man said. "Well, that's hardly a

defense now, is it?" He stood up and wiped some crumbs off his belly and onto the floor before walking around the front of the desk and sitting on the corner of it.

"Do you know who I am, Evan?"

I nodded, looking up at the man.

"And do you know what I do here, Evan?"

Again, I nodded.

"So, you understand that I have two lists: One for nice boys and girls, and one for naughty boys and girls, right?"

Another nod.

"Which list do you think you were on yesterday?"

I shrugged, hoping that he would just tell me. And hoping that it was the 'nice' list.

"Oh, come on Evan," he said. "You're going to have to start speaking up at some point." And then he stopped to think for a moment and hopped down from his desk. "I know what it is. I haven't properly introduced myself, have I? Well then," he extended his hand, "the name's Santa Claus."

I shook his hand and said, "E-E-Evan."

"I know," he winked. "Evan, what do you say we go someplace a little more comfortable to discuss your situation?" He moved toward a door to the left of his desk and said, "Follow me."

8

I followed Santa through the door. It led to a long corridor that was just as wide as it was long. There was a lot of noise, the sounds of industrial strength fans, and power tools and the chatter of people busily working away.

As I brought my eyes down from the high ceilings and began to get used to the noise, I noticed the elves — hundreds of them, possibly thousands. All were dressed in the same green outfits as the four I'd met when I came woke up earlier. And all were operating different levels of machinery and working together to make the world's supply of toys for yet another year.

I was overcome by joy when I saw this. The excitement of so many Christmas Eves and Christmas Mornings and Decembers of anticipation came rushing into my heart. And here I was, standing in the toy shop itself, watching thousands of toys being built all at once.

"It's a bit bigger than most people imagine," Santa said looking down at me. "I can tell by the look on your face that you probably expected some little log cabin out in the middle of a snowy wood. Well, that may have gotten the job done in years past, but the need for toys has grown, so has the need for us to grow to satisfy the demand."

I nodded absently, wanting to listen to what he was saying, but finding it impossible so long as I was standing in this Mecca of all kid-dom.

"So, do you want to see how it's all done?"

I nodded and began walking.

The first elves we stopped to watch were building electric guitars.

"How's it going Henry?" Santa stopped to ask an elf with a clipboard.

"Not bad, sir. Not bad at all. We got a good jump on these this year. Starting before Halloween was a good call on your part. It looks like we'll have some time to actually enjoy this Christmas Eve, rather than rushing around trying to finish the last batch of guitars."

"That's what I like to hear," Santa said, nodding, his arms crossed in front of his chest, clearly pleased with the way the elves had taken his suggestion and run with it. "Keep up the good work."

He patted Henry on the back twice and we moved onto the next group of elves, who were working like crazy on what Santa called, 'an old favorite.'

"Only about twenty thousand more Etcha-Sketches left to go," said another elf with a clipboard.

Santa nodded. "How many were on the list this year?"

"About two million, world-wide. Over one million of those are going to kids in the continental United States. And about half of those are the mini version."

Santa again nodded. "Isn't that funny, how this still intrigues them so."

"It is indeed," said the elf. "But that's okay. This is one toy that's easy to make."

Santa turned to me and said, "For time's sake, let's go ahead and skip right to electronics. I know that's what you're really interested in anyway."

He was right. I had written my letter to Santa over a month ago. In the envelope with the letter, I'd included a small list of six to eight items I was hoping Santa would bring me. When I say small, they were physically diminutive, but all of them cost a pretty penny. Cell phones, laptops, gaming consoles, iPads, iPods — they all cost a lot of money.

And now Santa was taking me to part of his 'workshop,' if that's even what he called this place, to see where all the really cool stuff was made.

We'd walked for a while when I asked, "Are we there yet?"

My legs were starting to get tired and I hadn't seen anything that so much as resembled an iPad.

"Be patient," Santa said. "You'll be glad you did."

After what seemed like a mile and a half, we arrived at the back wall of the industrial sized factory of a workshop where all of the electronic gadgets were made.

As we approached, I noticed that the process for assembling these more expensive gifts seemed much more involved. Up front there had been maybe five or six elves putting the toys together, with one clipboard holding supervisor. But back here there had to have been at least fifty elves gathering parts, and two elves assembling the item, with three elves to supervise each of the assemblers and five elves to supervise the parts gatherers.

"You've seen an iPad before, I assume," Santa said as we approached the assembly area.

I nodded that I had.

"Well, this is how it's done. There are hundreds of distinct parts, all of which have to be put in place meticulously, lest the device not work when Johnny or Suzy takes it out of the box on Christmas morning. We only have two elves skilled enough to assemble all of the parts correctly. And they had to go through hours of training and months of practice to get it just right."

I wanted to nod, but I found myself transfixed at the whole system. Everyone had a job to do, and even with all of the elves working in this little area, everyone knew exactly where to go so that things ran smoothly.

"Do you know why I brought you back here?" Santa said, looking down at me over the top of his glasses.

I had no idea, so I shrugged my shoulders. I was secretly hoping that Santa was going to allow me to spend some time here to learn how these amazing devices were made, or maybe even better — maybe he was going to give me a brand new iPad, right there on the spot!

"Not to worry," he said with a smile. And then he stood up on his tip toes and pointed to an elf in the back. He yelled, "Klous!" and the elf gave a slight nod of his head, delivered his part to the iPad assembler and joined us outside of the assembly area.

Even as Klous left his post, I could see that they had a system in place for replacing him, so that nothing ever stopped or got jammed up. For the first time, I noticed a line of elves on each side. When Klous had to leave, the first elf in this line up waited for the vacant spot by Klous to get to him, and then he hopped in and picked up where Klous had left off. It was brilliant.

"Klous," Santa said, "I want you to meet Evan."

Klous tipped his head in my direction and said, "Nice to meet you, Evan."

Santa then turned toward one of the supervising elves and said, "Den, I'm going to take Klous with me for a little while. I trust that you'll be alright without him."

The elf with the clipboard nodded, and Santa directed us to a side door, and out of the workshop.

9

I was taken aback by the smell that hit me when we walked through the door. All of the smells thus far had been sweet and wonderful, mixtures of cinnamon and clove and nutmeg and peppermint. It was like being surrounded by candy canes and apple pies. But the smell that met my nose was more like —

"Reindeer poop," Santa said with a cruel smile on his face. "Remember that Klous?"

Klous nodded, "Certainly do boss…and I don't miss it, that's for sure."

Santa said, "You're probably both wondering why we're standing here in the barn surrounded by the lovely smells of Reindeer droppings."

I most certainly was interested in what we were doing

in here, but I also had a feeling that it might be best if I didn't find out.

I was correct.

"Evan," Santa said, "Klous used to work in here every day. This was his first job here at the North Pole. And do you know what he did?"

"No," I said, not really wanting to know.

"Klous, how about you grab that shovel over there and give young Evan here a quick demonstration."

"Absolutely, boss," Klous said as he grabbed the shovel and a five gallon plastic bucket.

I watched in disgust as Klous walked over to the back side of one of the reindeer and shoveled the poop from the hay covered floor into the bucket. As if that wasn't bad enough, he leaned the shovel against a wooden beam and picked up the bucket and brought it over to a large rectangle in the floor. It was filled with water and looked like a giant swimming pool — but it smelled like a giant toilet.

There was a box attached to a nearby wall and Klous reached into the box and pulled out a pair of long rubber gloves. He then proceeded to tip the bucket upside down over the water, reach his hand into the bucket and scoop the poop out.

"Blitzen's been getting his share of fiber, I'd say," Klous said with a smile. "That batch was pretty squishy."

"Thank you for the demonstration Klous. You may go

take a shower and enjoy the rest of the day. You will report to work again tomorrow morning," Santa said.

"Oh, thank you boss. Thank you so much." Klous peeled off the glove and put it in the trash and ran out of the reindeer barn toward some well earned time off.

"His supervisor won't be happy with me, but that's okay. He'll find a way to manage without Klous. Great worker, that one," Santa said. He looked down at me. "Do you know why we're in here, Evan?"

I shook my head.

"Well, let's think about this for a second. You went against your parents wishes and ended up here, right."

I nodded.

"And you're aware by now that I have two lists, right?"

Again, I nodded.

"And you want to be on the 'nice' list, right?"

I gulped.

"We are one week away from Christmas. And I can't just drop what I'm doing to take you home. We have deadlines we're trying to meet here, as you've seen. And your actions have put you squarely on the 'naughty' list. And I know, you don't want to stay on the 'naughty' list, do you?"

I shook my head.

"So, just like Klous when he first started working here, this is your job for the next week. You will work here until Christmas Eve. Don't worry, I'll call your parents and let them know where you are. I'll tell them you're safe and I'll tell them you'll be here for the week."

Santa grabbed the shovel and handed it to me.

He walked to the door and before he stepped out said, "It's the week before Christmas, so we're feeding them a double portion every meal, to get their energy up."

And then he was gone.

And I was alone with my thoughts, and eight steaming piles of reindeer plop.

*a*fter a few moments, the smell had become easier to tolerate. I no longer found myself wanting to gag and throw up. It had become a mere nuisance and that was good enough for me.

It had never before occurred to me that cleaning up after eight reindeer would be an all day job. I'd always just assumed that someone might have to stop by their stall in the morning, and then again before bed each night. Actually, I'd never really thought about it at all... until this moment.

But now that I was in the middle of this stink fest, I couldn't believe the volume these guys could produce. I'd finish cleaning up one and move onto another, and keep doing that until I'd worked my way all the way around to where I'd began. And things were as bad — if not worse — than when I had started.

In total, that first day, I'd made my way around the barn seven times, working just as hard on the last trip around as I had on the first. What made it even worse, was that I didn't get there until about noon on that first day. And if Santa was planning on having me do this for the whole week, I'd surely have to be in here much earlier in the morning than that.

I stopped for a second to do the math and realized it was very possible that I could potentially make fourteen, or even as many as sixteen trips around here tomorrow.

That thought alone was enough to make me want to give up.

I hung my head and rested on the clean end of the shovel.

"Looks like you did well in here today," the deep voice of Santa boomed from behind me.

He'd startled me and I turned around, my face flushed red from embarrassment and having been caught resting on the job.

"Why don't you put that shovel down and follow me," he said with a smile. "Mrs. Claus has cooked us up some-thing wonderful."

I smiled and walked with him out of the barn. As we reached the door, he wrapped a blanket around me.

"It gets cold in these parts this time of year," he said with a wink.

And for the first time since I'd crashed here, I knew things were going to be okay.

$\mathcal{I}$ felt a little ridiculous sitting at Santa's dinner table dressed like an elf. But since I hadn't packed any clothes of my own for the journey, and I'd needed a shower in the worst way after leaving the reindeer, it was the best I could get.

And I guess if it was good enough for the elves, it was good enough for me.

I will say that the clothes were very comfortable. They were made of the softest velvet I'd ever felt in my whole life. And they smelled like fresh picked mint that smelled even better than the stuff my mom uses from the grocery store.

It was a little awkward sitting there at the dinner table with Santa. I had always thought that every night at the North Pole would be a huge feast, and that Santa and the elves would eat together and it would just be a big party all the time.

But as I sat down, Santa informed me that the elves all have their own homes and families to go home to when they're done at the workshop for the day. He told me that they all lived nearby in a little village that had been built just for them. And he said that it was least he could do for all that they did for him. "After all," he said, "I get all the glory, but they do the lion's share of the work."

As he finished telling me this, Mrs. Claus brought out a dutch oven full of stew. It was rich and delicious, full of carrots, onions, and earthy herbs. There was some kind of meat in it, but I didn't care to ask what it was. And she served it to us over mashed potatoes, with a biscuit on the side and a nice, tall glass of milk.

To say I was in heaven was an understatement. A few days ago, the thought of one of my friends sitting down and having a private dinner with Santa and Mrs. Claus would have made me too jealous to even speak of. And now, here I was, watching Santa pick flecks of carrot and biscuit out of his beard while Mrs. Claus laughed at him.

We didn't really talk about much during the meal. It tasted so good that I just shoveled it in without so much as a thought crossing my mind. I made a few noises of approval, mostly grunts and slurps, which made Mrs. Claus smile and giggle.

When dinner had concluded, Santa helped Mrs. Claus

to the kitchen with the dirty dishes. He came back to the table and sat down a moment later.

"She's fixing up something great for dessert," he said, patting his belly. "You're going to love it. Mrs. Claus is quite the cook, if I do say so myself."

"The stew was excellent," I said. I was beginning to feel a little more comfortable, as one tends to do when they've been in a new and strange place for a while. I knew that I would never feel totally comfortable here on the North Pole, but as long as I was here, I might as well make the most of it and get some conversations in with Santa and the elves.

"Yes, indeed," Santa said, sitting back in his chair and closing his eyes as he folded his hands and brought them to rest of top of his stomach. "After dessert you'll go upstairs and go to bed."

Well, I thought to myself, so much for conversation. Apparently I was still working my way off the 'naughty' list. And that meant an early bedtime.

"We have a spare bed up there that I think you'll find adequate," Santa explained. "For the longest time I told Mrs. Claus that we didn't need one. I argued with her for a couple of weeks anyway, telling her there was no way anyone would ever find their way up here for a visit. As long as I can remember, it's always been us who've done the traveling." He sat up for a moment and opened his eyes. "Of course, had I been a little more attentive to things, I might have seen you coming."

I giggled nervously. "Yeah, sorry about that."

"Evan, I'm happy to hear that you're sorry. But, I'm not the one who needs the apology, am I?"

And for the first time since I'd arrived at the North Pole, it hit me. I hadn't thought about my parents once since I'd been here. Santa was absolutely right. As soon as I got home I'd make sure that I told my parents I was sorry.

Mrs. Claus interrupted my thoughts by bursting through the door with the most decadent looking cake I'd ever seen. She set it down on the table and cut into it effortlessly. A gigantic slice was cut for Santa, who had a large smile on his face at the sight of the triangular slice of spongy chocolate goodness.

She served me next, giving me a much smaller piece than she'd given Santa. And then she sat down in her chair with a cup of tea and nothing more.

"You aren't having any?" I asked.

"Oh, heavens no," she said, blushing a little. "As I get older, it gets harder and harder to keep the weight off. I've found it best not to put it on in the first place."

I nodded and smiled, thinking that Mrs. Claus and my mother would have so much to talk about if they were to ever meet.

By the time I took my first bite, Santa was holding his

plate out for more. Mrs. Claus smiled as she put another slice on his plate.

"It's nice to know that after all these years, my cooking still satisfies you."

He just nodded and dove into the second piece of chocolate cake.

As I lifted my fork to my mouth, I noticed little slices of cherries in the cake. And I smiled, thinking that this is a special little morsel of information that only I know about.

Well, me and Mrs. Claus.

12

*a*fter dinner, Santa told me I could stay up a little later if I did the dishes. Otherwise it was right to bed.

If I'd have been home and it would have been my father making that deal with me, I probably would have gone right to bed.

But I wasn't home. I was at the North Pole. I was in Santa's house. Of course, I was going to do the dishes.

Honestly, it wasn't any different than doing the dishes at home. Their kitchen was a little bigger than my parents' kitchen. But they were basically the same: sink, counters, stove, refrigerator, cupboards and cabinets, and lots of dirty dishes that needed to be washed.

Once I'd dried and stacked the last dish on the

counter, Santa walked me up to my room and showed me where some extra blankets were, in case I got cold.

"You're not used to the cold nights up here. You may need to cover up a little extra." He stood in the doorway and said, "I was going to wait until tomorrow morning to tell you this, but I'd feel bad sending you to bed thinking that you were going to be cleaning after the reindeer tomorrow. Honestly, we have a machine that does all that now. As a matter of fact, Klous invented it." He smiled at the thought of Klous. Santa certainly had a sweet spot in his heart for that particular elf.

"What am I going to be doing?" I asked.

"Goodnight," Santa smiled, closing the door behind him without telling me.

I wasn't sure how to feel. I thought, perhaps, it was a good thing that I wouldn't be working in the barn the next day.

But then a thought occurred to me as I tried to get to sleep. It was one of my father's favorite expressions, and it kept me awake. He was fond of saying, 'It could always be worse.'

The way my father had used it, had always been to get me to look on the bright side. I'd come home from school and complained about another kid, or a lesson the teacher had wanted me to work on, and my father would swoop in and say, "Well, Evan, it could always be worse." It was his way of telling me that I didn't have it so bad and that

I should accept whatever challenge was in front of me and be thankful that I had it so good.

As I lay in bed and the darkness overtook the room, I thought about my mom and dad. I thought about how horrible I'd been to them and the dumb thing I'd done. I felt tears rush into my eyes and roll down my cheek. For the first time in years, I cried myself to sleep.

And for the first time all day, I wanted to go home.

13

I heard a knock at the door and I could feel the light tap, tap, tapping on my eyelids, telling them quite forcefully that it was time to wake up and see what the day had in store for me.

"Wakey, wakey," Santa said, throwing open the door. He was holding a new elf outfit on a clothes hanger, which he hung from the door handle on the inside of the door. "Put this on and be downstairs with your teeth brushed, your face washed, and your hair combed in ten minutes."

I sat up slowly.

"You're going to have to move faster than that," he said before shutting the door. As he walked down the hall, I could hear his booming voice, "Only a few more days until Christmas Eve. Lots to do! Lots to do!"

I slid off the bed and took off last nights slept in elf clothes and placed them at the foot of the bed. Then I put on the newly pressed and super minty smelling new set of clothes that Santa had left for me.

Mrs. Claus had put out a toothbrush, damp washcloth, and wet comb for me. There was a note next to the toothbrush.

Evan,

I heard you crying last night before I went to bed.

In a few days, this week will be a happy memory for you.

Try to enjoy it.

Your parents know where you are and they know you're safe.

Mrs. C

I SMILED and slipped the note into my pocket, happy that she had taken the time to write it. She was right, these few days would be a happy memory for me someday. Even though Santa was going to have me working my way back onto the 'nice' list from the 'naughty' list, there was a lot I could learn while I was here. And there were definitely some happy memories to be made.

With that thought in my mind, I did my morning grooming and headed downstairs to face the day and enjoy it...no matter what.

14

"*You* ou want me to do what?" I asked. And I knew the moment I said it that I was out of line. But I was also cold and still a little groggy.

"You heard me," Santa said. "And let's face it, you haven't made it off that 'naughty' list yet."

He handed me a shovel and walked away.

I stood there in the cold and the wind, equipped with a new parka, heavy scarf, and heated gloves.

The task of shoveling off the entire runway so that Santa and the reindeer would be able to take off on Christmas Eve seemed like an incredibly daunting task.

Before he'd left, Santa pointed out a few red and green stakes that outlined the shape of the runway, so that I didn't end up shoveling grass and wasting my time.

It had to be at least a hundred feet to the end, if not more. And it was no less than twenty feet wide. And the snow was up past my knees.

I'd have rather been in the barn cleaning up poop and scooping it out of a bucket, I thought to myself.

Then I heard my father's voice in my head, saying, "It could always be worse."

I nodded and put the shovel into the snow.

After five minutes or so, an elf appeared, seemingly out of nowhere. He was dressed as I was and had a shovel of his own.

"Name's Bert," he said. "You've passed the first five minute milestone, so the big man sent me out to help."

I smiled. "Thank you," I said.

And then another elf appeared.

"Name's Glenn," he said. "Mr. Claus said you've just passed the gratitude milestone, so I'm here to help."

Bert and Glenn started shoveling and I stood there watching them. I was completely dumbfounded and amazed.

And then the thought occurred to me, that if I said the words 'thank you' and Glenn showed up, maybe I could do it again and have even more help. It was worth a try.

"Thank you, thank you, thank you, thank you," I said, figuring that six elves and myself would be enough to get this job done.

But when I finished saying my last 'thank you,'

Glenn was gone, and so was Bert. And all the snow they'd just shoveled had been put back on the runway, and it looked as though it had never been shoveled at all.

"Evan." I heard Santa's booming voice behind me. I turned around and there he was, standing in the middle of everything with not so much as a single footprint around him. "Do not try to get out of this. It is important to do things because they are good for others. You must learn to do things less for yourself."

I stared at him blankly, not fully understanding what he was saying.

"Do you understand what I'm telling you?"

I shook my head.

"Bert appeared to you because you started shoveling the runway. You were not doing that for yourself. You were doing it for me, for my reindeer, for all of the boys and girls who need this snow to be removed so that we can get around the world on Christmas Eve."

"Okay," I said. "And when I said 'thank you' the first time, I was showing that I was truly thankful for Bert's help and so Glenn showed up. But when I tried to get more help, I was doing that for me. And so they both disappeared and left me alone."

Santa winked and said, "You've got it, Evan. A selfish life is a lonely life. But a life lived in service of others is fulfilling."

I understood what he was trying to say to me, thought not entirely. That would come later, no doubt.

"Thank you, Santa," I said. And it was genuine. And I was grateful for the lesson.

I started to shovel and Bert and Glenn showed back up.

It took us all day to shovel the runway, but the three of us had a great time and shared much laughter together.

When we'd finished, Santa came to get me and we walked back to his house through the cold. And Mrs. Claus had prepared another wonderful feast.

We ate dinner together and we were satisfied because we knew our work was helping others, and that others would be happy as a result.

That night I had the best night of sleep.

15

I woke up sore before Santa could wake me. The light was coming through my window again, but I could tell that it was still early.

When I sat up on my bed, my soreness, which had been apparent while I was lying down, became almost burdensome. My lower back and upper arms felt like they were on fire and the pain I was feeling in both forced me to sit on the edge of the bed longer than normal.

As I sat there, I could feel a tingling in my thighs and I knew that when I put my feet on the floor I was going to have some trouble walking.

Slowly, I slid to the edge of the bed and put my toes to the floor and began the process of gently lowering myself. I was careful not to go too fast, and I wanted to have both feet flat against the carpet before I put any weight on them.

As expected, there was pain. But it wasn't where I thought it would be. Instead of being concentrated in my thighs, I could feel it in my calves and hips. And the pain was different. My calves had a tightness about them, like someone was tugging a rope inside my leg and I was having difficulty tugging it back.

My hips on the other hand felt like people were taking turns throwing golf balls at me. Every step brought sharp pain.

I limped over to the closet, where I'd seen Mrs. Claus go the first night to get me a clean change of clothes. I opened the door and the smell of fresh mint bowled me over, bringing a smile to my face and a much needed blast of awesome to my day.

Eventually, my movement proved to win out in the battle between my body and its pain. I was still sore, but I could now move a little better and felt as though I would be ready for any task Santa put in front of me.

With a smile on my face and a new minty-fresh outfit, I headed downstairs to see what the day would bring

16

*W*hen I came downstairs, Santa was already sitting at the table and Mrs. Claus was pouring him a cup of hot coffee. He was reading the newspaper, scrunching his nose every so often and humming his approval or disapproval at what he was reading. Occasionally he'd let out a, "Can you believe that guy?" or, "Some people," before turning to the next page.

Mrs. Claus said, "Good morning, Evan."

"Good morning," I said as I sat at my usual spot. I don't know if you've ever had a 'usual spot' somewhere you'd least expected, but for me, having my usual spot at Santa's dining room table was pretty awesome, even if it was only for a few more days.

"We are having a simple breakfast today," she said. "There's so much work to do, we want to keep our tummies light. Would you like some toast or oatmeal with strawberries?"

"Toast please," I answered.

Santa put the paper down after Mrs. Claus had gone back into the kitchen to get my breakfast. I watched as he folded it just like my dad, bringing the top to the bottom and then folding the right side to the left and setting a neat rectangular vessel of news down next to his empty toast plate.

"We have a very busy couple of days," he said to me. "With Christmas Eve almost here, it's going to be all hands on deck. Today you will be working directly with the elves, sorting toys and getting everything organized for Christmas delivery."

I nodded and felt a growth of excitement deep within myself. I was going to be helping with the magical part of Christmas. I would not be shoveling reindeer leavings or snow off the runway. I would be right there, elbow to elbow with Santa's elves, helping to get things ready for the big man himself!

"I had a feeling I'd see that smile on your face, Evan. I just want to let you know that it's not the easiest task in the world. You have to be careful, and thoughtful, and it's going to be physically difficult as well. You were sore this morning, weren't you?"

"Yes," I said.

"Well, today and tomorrow's work will make your

body feel the same way. Your muscles will burn and your joints will ache. But this work will also test your mind and your eyes as well. There's a lot of pressure to get the toys in the right place, so that things go smoothly during delivery. A lot of people think that I just have a big satchel of toys that fits in my sleigh, but it's much more than that."

I nodded, feeling like I was up for the challenge, but still nervous that it might be too much.

"Let me ask you something," Santa said, leaning in. "Have any of your friends ever asked the question, 'How does he fit all the toys for the world in his sleigh?'"

"All the time. None of us can figure it out."

He sat back and smiled, folding his arms over his belly and breathing deeply.

"As soon as you finish your breakfast, you'll know."

a s we walked to the workshop, the wind and cold slapping at my cheeks, I still felt hungry. One piece of toast just didn't seem like enough. But I knew we'd be working hard in a few moments and I wouldn't even have time to think about my hunger until dinner.

Santa got to the door and put his thumb to a sensor on the door and the door opened.

"After you," he said, allowing me to step through the door first.

Once he was in, I followed him through a few hallways and into a mammoth warehouse. The floor was made of cement and stretched for what looked like at least a mile in length and width. There were little square markings on the floor, each with the first and last name of someone, their age and an address. Each square was about three feet wide and three feet long.

"This is one of our sorting houses," Santa explained. "In just a few minutes…" he looked at his watch, "four to be exact, this room will be filled with five hundred elves. The door on the far end will open and the toys that have been made and sorted will be waiting to be sorted again. It will be cold at first, but you'll be moving so much that after five or ten minutes you'll be wishing we could open the other doors as wide."

I stood there, mouth agape, unsure what to say. I found enough of a voice to ask, "Are these all the kids in the whole world?"

"Oh, heavens no," Santa chuckled. "This is one of forty such warehouses that we have on the premise. One of the perks of working way up here, is that no one wants to live up here. So we have lots of room to do our work. And we need it. Actually this warehouse, here, is for region 5 E. All of the toys that are sorted here will be going to Canada and the Central United States."

I could hear a loud noise, dull and heavy, growing louder.

Santa looked down at me and smiled.

"Here they come."

atching the elves emerge was like watching a military exercise. They came in through a wide door to our right, marching in twenty five rows of twenty, stopping in the center of the warehouse and turning to face Santa.

Santa stepped up and pulled a microphone from his pocket. He flicked a switch on the side to the 'On' position and looked up toward the ceiling, where four speakers had been hung. He tapped the top of the microphone and gave a gentle blow of air into the top of it, which was heard through the speakers. Then he nodded and looked behind us to the left, where an elf with a clipboard was standing. Santa gave the elf a thumbs up, which the elf returned before disappearing through a small door.

"A minute early!" Santa's voice boomed through the speakers. "Thank you and good morning."

In unison the elves returned, "Good morning to you Santa."

"It is truly wonderful to have such a dedicated and professional group as yourselves working to make Christmas as great as it can be for every child in the world. As you know, this is the first of forty such speeches I will be making in the next hour. I will be brief as we all have much work to do.

"I would like Benny, Wally, Vicky, Jerry, and Val to please step forward."

Five elves emerged from the group and walked toward Santa and me. I recognized the one named Benny from my first day here, but I was seeing the others for the first time.

Santa continued, "These five individuals are your EICs. If you have any questions, you find one of them. Things need to run as smoothly as possible. I have selected these five EICs for region 5 E to ensure that that happens. Most of you have done this before and you always do a wonderful job. And you know the deal: If we have another perfect year for your region, you will get a fantastic bonus and some well earned time off!"

The elves cheered a deafening cheer at this last proclamation.

"Have a very productive two days everyone, and thank

you in advance." Santa turned off the microphone and a tiny click came through the speakers.

The doors on the other side of the warehouse began to open and a rush of cold air filled the room. Some of the elves stood tall and strong and did not move until the doors were fully open. And then they made their way to the wall of toys that was waiting for them. Others huddled together or hugged themselves and jumped up and down to keep warm before moving toward the toys.

I was cold, but I didn't want to show it. So I stood there, next to Santa, straight as an arrow with my teeth chattering loudly in my head.

Santa turned to the EICs and told them, "This is Evan. He will be working here with you today. Benny, you have the most experience with Evan. Please see to it that he learns the ropes and contributes to the work. And make sure you touch base with me later tonight to tell me how he did."

"Yes, sir," Benny said.

Santa said, "Thanks for getting everyone here on time. I'm hopeful that the other regions will be as punctual as you...though I'm doubtful about 4 B. They've been late getting started three years in a row. It's a good thing they know what they're doing," Santa winked.

And with that, he was gone.

And I was standing with Benny, waiting to find out how this all worked.

19

*B*enny put a finger in the air and said, "Hold on just a sec, Evan, okay?"

I nodded and watched as Benny ran back to a desk along the front wall of the warehouse. The other EICs were standing there too. They had each picked up a plastic package and opened it. I couldn't see everything, but from where I was standing it looked like the each had a bright red outfit with a green hat, a name tag and clipboard. There were some other things as well, but they were small and the EICs put them into the pockets of their new red uniform. And I figured that if Benny wanted me to know what was in his package, he'd have invited me over to have a look.

He walked back over to me and said, "Alright, Evan." He pointed to the floor in front of us. "This is a step by step process. We have the floor divided into four areas. Basically all of those toys are labeled with four different labels. We read the white label first. That white label will have a number on it: One, two, three, or four. If you look up toward the ceiling, you can now see the number One hanging above us. This is number one quadrant. All of the white labels with a one go here. Do you understand?"

I nodded.

"Good," he said. "Then he pointed out the other three quadrants and said, "Just check the white label for now and help get those toys into those four groups. That'll take us most of today, then we'll break up into quadrant groups and sort the smaller groups of toys into yet smaller groups. But I'll tell you about that later."

"Okay."

"Do you have any questions?" Benny asked.

"Just one."

"What's that?"

"What's an EIC?"

"Oh that," Benny smiled. "Santa loves his acronyms. It means Elf In Charge. So, we have the red suits that smell like cinnamon candies instead of the green ones that smell like mint. It makes us easier to find if you have a question. You ask us a question, and we will answer it. That's our job."

"Okay," I said.

There was an awkward silence as I waited for Benny

to say something further, but he didn't. He gave me a strange look like he didn't understand why I was there.

"Should I just go do this now?" I asked.

He nodded.

With my mind no longer on how empty my stomach was, but rather on hoping that I didn't throw up from nervousness, I set off on the long walk to the wall of toys.

$\mathcal{I}$ stood there staring at it.

On either side of me, elves were coming in and picking away at the wall of wrapped gifts and carrying them off to their properly labeled quadrant.

But not me. Not yet. There are some things in this world that you just have to stand in front of and stare at for a few moments. This was one of those things. For a kid, there would be no more beautiful a sight than a wall of wrapped Christmas presents that stretched hundreds of feet wide and fifty feet tall, and who knows how far back. There were elves on ladders, and elves operating cranes to get the toys down to elves on the floor.

The colors of the wrapping paper came together to make the Christmas gift equivalent of a modern art masterpiece. And I was transfixed in its beauty.

The smell of cinnamon candy entered my nose, enhancing this moment...until I realized that Benny was standing right next to me.

I looked at him and he was looking at his clipboard, writing something down.

"Rumor has it, you're on the 'naughty' list and you're desperately trying to work your way back onto the 'nice' list. Now, Santa hasn't said anything to anybody, per se. But he has had you doing chores around here that have been reserved for similar situations in the past. And you're not really doing anything wrong right now, staring at this mammoth load of work we've got in front of us. But you're not really doing anything good right now, either. And, so long as I've been here, the way to get off the 'naughty' list and back onto the 'nice' list is to do some serious acts of good."

He finished writing what he was writing and then looked me in the eye as he turned around and walked away.

I caught his not so subtle drift and grabbed a present from the bottom of the wall. The white label read 'one' and I began my long walk over to number one quadrant.

The walk was incredibly long, and though the present I'd chosen wasn't heavy, by the end of the journey it had become cumbersome.

Putting it down, I felt a quick sense of relief at completing my first goal. Then, I looked down the line and realized that I would have to go back and do this again.

I put my head down and began the journey.

When I'd reached the wall of presents, I heard laughter and snickers. A lot of them.

Benny was standing there with his arms crossed and a satisfied smile on his face. "I think I may have skipped a step in the directions." And here he took a second to guffaw before continuing. "You see, Santa would not have devised this method of doing things, only to have us walk a mile one way with one present at a time."

I looked around, realizing now that I'd done the wrong thing and had not been very observant. The other elves were taking presents and stacking them onto labeled pallets. As the pallets filled up, an elf in a fork lift would take the pallet to the proper quadrant, where the presents would stay until step two was started.

I laughed. What else could I do? Sure, I felt like an idiot, but with all of the things I'd been introduced to over the past few days, it never even occurred to me that walking presents from one end of the warehouse to another might be looked at by Santa as less than efficient.

Without so much as another word, Benny walked away and left me to my work. I took a deep breath, picked up a present and checked the white tag. It had a number three on it. I walked it to the number three pallet that was located about twelve feet from where I was standing and put the present down.

When I got back to the wall of gifts I was much less tired than I'd been the first time.

I just had to smile about it and grab another present.

$\mathcal{N}$ow, I have to level with you about a few things. As you have probably already realized, you are learning about things that no one else has ever learned of before.

I hope that you might be as excited about reading about these things as I was about experiencing them firsthand.

When I originally talked to Santa about writing this story down and sharing it with other people, he seemed less than thrilled. He figured I would just share it with some of my friends and that would be it.

And he knows how people are. It's like playing a game of 'telephone.' Even if I'd told my friends everything, the likelihood of them telling other people exactly as it happened would be small. And eventually, it would turn into something like this:

> "And I have a friend, who has this friend who went to the North Pole. And he says that Santa's suit is made out of cinnamon candies and that the elves have a giant forklift that clears the reindeer poop off the runway. And this elf, Lenny, was in charge of making sure that all of the presents got wrapped the right way - and they did it right in the middle of a giant pool while they ate toast and cherry cake."

So, as you can clearly see, Santa's secrets would be in no danger whatsoever of being found out by everyone. But nowadays, with the internet and books on electronic devices and such, Santa was afraid that my little tell-all book might make it difficult to keep his secrets his.

And I can't really say that I blame him.

I will tell you that all of the information you've read so far is true to my experience. All of those things really happened to me. And it was wonderful and scary and magical and amazing. And Santa's a pretty great guy for letting me include that much in the story.

But when I sent him the manuscript for this book, he called me and said that I had to make some cuts. He said that I could keep everything in the story up until this part. But everything from the final three gift sortings to the actual delivery of presents was off limits.

I probably shouldn't tell you this, but I know you're dying to know. And I'm willing to go on the 'naughty' list again just to tell you.

The whole bag on the sleigh thing. It's really quite ingenious how he does it. Those forty warehouses that he had all the gifts in are set up by region. And those squares with the kids names and addresses on them are like little tele-porters. That means, when Santa's in his sleigh, all he has to do is press the right button at the right time and the gifts on any given square are sent directly to his sleigh instantly. It's almost like magic pixie dust, but so much cooler.

So that means the gifts that end up under your tree on Christmas aren't actually in his sleigh until he gets to your house. That means they aren't exposed to the cold and the wind, or the rain and the snow. And they don't run the risk of falling out and smashing on the ground somewhere on the other side of the world. Plus, it's easier for the reindeer, which means they can fly faster and get Santa where he needs to go before the sun comes up!

That's really all I can tell you. And don't worry about me and that whole list thing. I told Santa already that I was going to tell you that part anyway. He wasn't too happy about it, but he said that as long as I didn't tell you how he really gets into your house nowadays, especially in the age of chimney-less homes, then I was in the clear.

Alright, now it's time to see how my journey ends. See you on the next page!

22

*I*t was Christmas Eve. My last day on the North Pole. I was really missing my parents now and couldn't wait to get home to see them. But I was sad that this would be my last day here. There aren't a lot of opportunities that come along in life that are as cool as this.

Santa had assured me that he would get me home in time to go to bed and wake up surprised on Christmas morning. And he told me specifically that he had purposely kept me out of the warehouse for my region, so that I could still be surprised on Christmas morning.

"Even though you know many of the inner workings now," he said to me, "there is still much you don't know. And that's the way it should be. Every child deserves to have that sense of wonder and awe on Christmas morning."

He'd said this to me over my last breakfast with him and Mrs. Claus. She had gone all out, making eggs and bacon, pancakes and donuts, and plenty of minty hot chocolate.

And she'd made sure that when I was finished with breakfast that she'd given me my clothes back for the journey home.

"We can't be sending you out of here looking like an elf after all," she'd said with a wink.

Honestly, I'd have totally been okay with it. But I had a feeling that they didn't want too many authentic items leaving the North Pole.

After I'd changed back into my regular Evan clothes, Santa brought me to his office. He sat behind his desk and I sat his that horrible chair that I'd sat on my first day there.

"Evan, it's been a real pleasure getting to know you. You're a fine young man and a hard worker. This week, you have more than made up for your mistake, so long as you truly apologize to your parents when you get home. And in the future, try to be more thoughtful about how they feel."

I nodded.

He opened one of his desk drawers and I heard the jingle of bells. When he pulled out his hand, he had a small silver bell. He stood up and walked around his desk, motioning me over to him.

I walked over, and for the first and only time in my life, I hugged Santa. I could feel that this was goodbye and had to fight the tears back. It was a long hug. And he rubbed my back. And then he gave me two pats and we backed away from one another.

He extended his hand to me and placed the bell in my hand.

"I want you to keep this. Keep it as a reminder of your time here. So long as you believe, it will ring for you."

"Thank you," I said. I didn't know what else to say.

"Be good," Santa told me before calling on Benny to see to it that I got home safely.

And with that, Santa and I parted ways and my week at the North Pole was over.

23

I'm not allowed to tell you how I got home. But I can tell you that I got home safely on Christmas Eve just in time for dinner.

My parents were excited to see me and wanted to know all about it. I told them everything I could remember and then we went to the early Christmas Eve church service before coming home and watching 'A Charlie Brown Christmas' and 'How the Grinch Stole Christmas.'

Before I went to bed that night, I apologized to my parents and they accepted. It seemed to me that either Santa or Mrs. Claus had really helped me out and smoothed things over with them. Normally, they'd have talked about all the reasons why what I'd done was wrong. But this time they just accepted my apology and tucked me in.

I fell asleep, too tired to even think about what the next morning would bring.

24

*W*hen I woke up, I could smell sausage, home fries and coffee coming from downstairs. The sun that normally shined in my window first thing in the morning, was not shining in at all. The sun was high in the sky and I noted that I must've slept in.

I put on my slippers and ran downstairs.

"Good morning, sleepy head," my father greeted me in the hallway. "Santa must've really put you to work these past few days."

I smiled and said, "He did."

"Do you want to see the tree?" my mother asked as she brought a cup of coffee, ready to spill over the edge, to her lips and slurped.

"Sounds like a plan!" I said as I rushed into the living

room and saw all sorts of beautifully wrapped presents and ribbons and bows. Many of them, I recognized as the handy wrapping of the elves. And some of them were the less than handy wrapping of my parents.

I smiled and jingled the bell in my pocket.

Before I could sit down, my father said, "Before we get too involved in here, why don't we go look in the garage."

I looked at him with a smirk, wondering what could possibly be out there for me.

I ran through the kitchen, toward the back door.

My mom yelled, "Evan, you need a coat!"

And I could hear my father calling her back, "It's okay, hun, he'll be okay for a few minutes."

I jumped down the steps two at a time and ran across the icy driveway. I put my hand on the freezing garage door handle and opened the door.

And when my eyes had adjusted to the darkness of the garage, I could see a brand new space ship. It was bigger than the one that Zebo'd given to me. It was metallic blue, with a perfect little cockpit, and what looked to be double reinforced sound proof glass for the hood.

I walked over to it and looked inside.

There was a card on the seat, my name on the envelope.

Finding the edge of the hatch, I opened the ship and reached down to grab the envelope. It even had that new space ship smell.

I opened the card and read:

Evan,

We tried to fix your old ship, but you really did a number on it when you crashed. The elves and I decided it would be best just to start over and build you a new one. You'll be interested to hear that this ship was personally designed by Klous and assembled by Benny in his spare time.

When you begin your next voyage to Pluto, remember to be safe…and remember to make sure that it works into your parents schedule before you go!

Merry Christmas,
    The Big Man
    Mrs. Claus
    Benny
    Klous
    And everyone from the North Pole

I TURNED to see my parents silhouetted in the doorway, my father's arm around my mom. I put the card down and hugged them.

"So, does this mean I can go to Pluto?" I asked.

"We'll discuss that later," said my dad. "Right now, we need to get inside before you catch a cold. Plus, there are more presents to open!"

Together, we walked inside to enjoy the best Christmas Ever!

WHO IS ZEBO?

 ear Readers,

I HOPE you've found **The Trip of a Lifetime** fun and exciting, interesting and heartwarming. Those were the emotions going through my mind and my heart as I wrote it.

Early in the book, Evan makes reference to an alien named Zebo, who gifted him a space ship so that Evan can travel through space.

Zebo did not come out of thin air — he came from another book...that I created from thin air. So, I guess Zebo did come out of thin air...but there is a Zebo story out there — yeah, that's what I'm trying to say!

Boy, I got confused for a moment there.

ANYWAY, if you'd like to know where Zebo came from, let me invite you check out my story Zack and Zebo. Just click on the book cover to read this story if you're reading this in an ebook. If you're reading this on paper, you can get this book in paperback too. It's one of my absolute favorites!

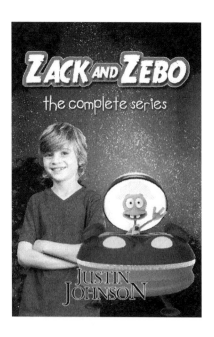

*T*hank you very much for reading my stories. I hope that you enjoy reading them as much as I enjoy writing them. If you'd like to contact me, I'd like to hear from you!

You must be 18 years or older!

MY EMAIL IS
middlegradeteacherwriter@gmail.com

IF YOU'D LIKE to get updates on new projects and discounts on books:
Sign Up for the Updates!

IF YOU'D LIKE to join my facebook group and get updates and interact with me that way, go to:
Middle Grade Teacher Writer

IF YOU'D LIKE to check out my website:
https://middlegradeteacherwriter.wordpress.com

*H*ere is my complete list of books as of the publication of this book. To find these books, click on the book title to go that book's page — or check out my Amazon Author Page by clicking here.

INDIVIDUAL BOOKS

- The Complete Coby Collins
- Zack and Zebo: The Complete Series
- The Jungle: The Complete Series
- Grade School Super Hero: The Complete Trilogy (Amazon Best Seller)
- Farty Marty and Other Stories (Amazon Best Seller)
- Do Not Feed the Zombies and Other Stories (Amazon Best Seller)
- The Disgusting and Heartwarming Collection
- Bunnyzilla
- Evan Copper Planet Hopper: Journey to Mercury
- Trip of a Lifetime (Amazon Best Seller)
- Frog

SCAB AND BEADS Mystery Series Books

- Scab and Beads: Locket's Away
- Scab and Beads: Milk Mayhem
- Scab and Beads: Homework Heist

BOOK COLLECTIONS

- Scab and Beads: Locket's Away, Milk Mayhem, Homework Heist
- Four Complete Fantasy Adventure Series (Coby Collins, Zack and Zebo, The Jungle, Grade School Super Hero)
- Three Complete Adventures and Three Complete Mysteries (Coby Collins, Zack and Zebo, Grade School Super Hero, Scab and Beads: Locket's Away, Milk Mayhem, and Homework Heist)
- Adventure Two Pack (Coby Collins and The Jungle)
- Adventure Two Pack (Coby Collins and Zack and Zebo)
- Adventure Two Pack (Coby Collins and Grade School Super Hero)
- Adventure Two Pack (Zack and Zebo and The Jungle)
- Adventure Two Pack (Zack and Zebo and Grade School Super Hero)
- Adventure Two Pack (Grade School Super Hero and The Jungle)

Made in the USA
Coppell, TX
15 November 2022